DISNEY'S
THE GREAT MOUSE DETECTIVE

BASIL'S GREAT ESCAPES

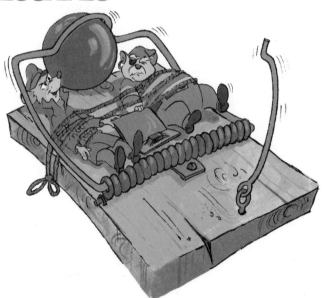

4

A GOLDEN BOOK • NEW YORK

Western Publishing Company, Inc., Racine, Wisconsin 53404

Basil of Baker Street, the brilliant mouse detective, was hot on the trail of Ratigan, who possessed the most evil criminal mind in England. Then Dr. David Q. Dawson showed up with young Olivia Flaversham, who wanted Basil to find her father. Her father had been kidnapped by the bat Fidget, one of Ratigan's gang.

Why Ratigan would kidnap a toymaker was puzzling. But it soon became clear that he was to be part of Ratigan's plot to overthrow the Mouse Queen of England by replacing her with a mechanical doll only Flaversham could make. Then Ratigan could rule the land.

Basil and Dawson, disguised as sailors, had tracked Ratigan to his den—only to be taken prisoners.

With Olivia helplessly corked up in a bottle, Ratigan
tied Basil and Dawson to a trap. He gloated, "I had so
many ingenious ideas of how to do away with the two of
you that I didn't know which to choose. So I decided to use
them all!

"Marvelous, isn't it?" he continued as he climbed a
ladder. He set the tone arm of a phonograph. He started
the turntable, setting in motion his evil scheme.

"Everything's ready. Oh, this is wicked, so delightfully wicked," Ratigan said to Fidget, as the two prisoners watched helplessly. Then he flew off in a toy dirigible to join the rest of the gang at the palace and surprise the queen.

"Bye–bye, Basil," Ratigan called. "Remember to smile for the camera."

As the record played, a long cord tied around the tone arm of the phonograph began to tighten.

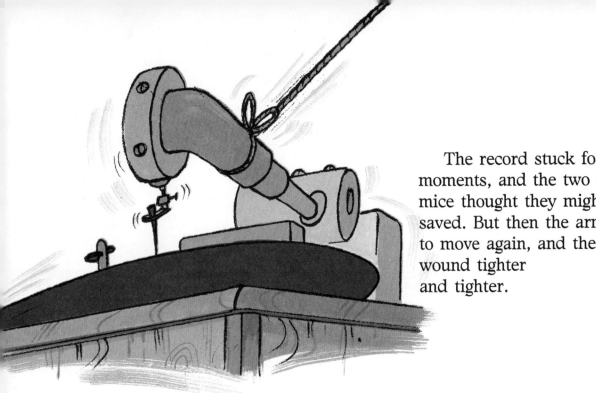

The record stuck for a few moments, and the two doomed mice thought they might be saved. But then the arm started to move again, and the cord wound tighter and tighter.

"It's finally happened," moaned Basil. "I've been outwitted, beaten, duped, made a fool of...."

"If you've given up," said Dawson, "why don't you just set off the trap now!"

"That's it!" exclaimed Basil, suddenly brightening.

Just then the cord yanked a cork out from under a wineglass, tipping it over. A ball was released into a funnel. Bouncing back and forth through lengths of winding pipe, the ball dropped out the bottom onto a ramp.

As Dawson watched the approaching ball with horror, Basil was doing some rapid calculations.

"Dawson," he said, "at the exact moment I tell you, we must release the trigger. Get ready....Now!"

At that very moment, Basil and Dawson pushed hard on the trigger of the trap. *Snap!* Just as the ball was about to hit the trigger, it got jammed in the bar.

The bar began to vibrate. So much pressure built up that it loosened a pin from the trap.

Ping! The pin went flying off into a gun that was all set up to fire.

Boom! As the gun fired, the pin knocked it off balance. The bullet went upward, off course.

Basil, grinning with joy, could hardly contain himself.

The bullet hit a crossbow, knocking *it* upward just as it was about to fire. *Twang!* The arrow shot off, hitting an ax and breaking its handle.

Whoosh! The ax spun around dizzily in the air and went off *its* course.

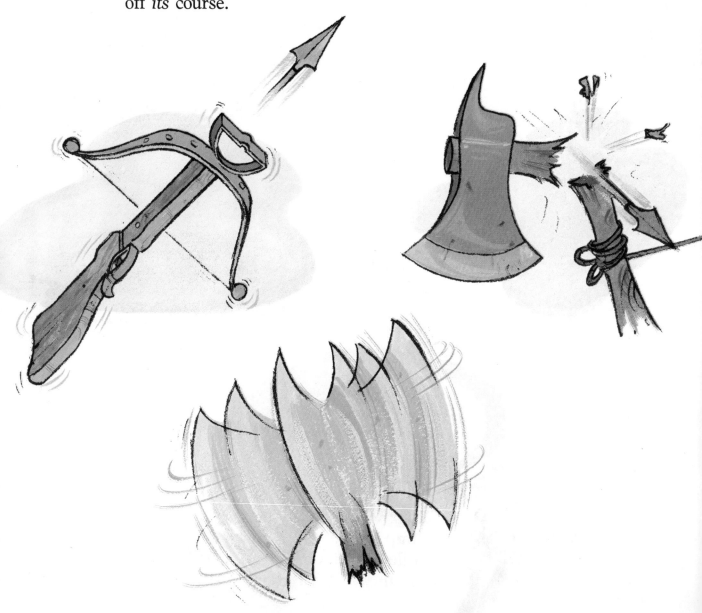

The ax came tumbling down directly between Basil and
Dawson, splitting the trap in two with a mighty *thwack!*
    The half with Basil flew off in one direction. The half
with Dawson flew off in the other direction.

An anvil that was supposed to have come down *splat!* on Basil and Dawson crushed the ax instead. As a final touch, a funeral wreath came floating down on top of the anvil.

Dawson was dazed by what had happened. But Basil rapidly jumped off the trap and changed out of his sailor disguise. Then, as a camera went off, he leaned in close to Dawson and flashed a wide grin.

Basil freed Olivia from her bottle. "Quickly," he said. "There's no time to lose." And the three mice took off for the palace to try to stop Ratigan.

At the palace, Basil succeeded in rescuing the queen from Ratigan's clutches. And he exposed Ratigan as a fiend.

But just when it looked as if Ratigan's days of crime were over, he seized Olivia and took off in his dirigible.

"Gather up those balloons!" commanded Basil, pointing to a cluster of them on the fence. Using the balloons as a dirigible air bag, he, Dawson, and Flaversham all took off after them.

As the dirigible streaked across the night sky toward
the Tower Bridge, Olivia taunted her captor. "Just wait.
Basil isn't through yet. He's not afraid of a big, old, ugly rat
like you!"

"Sit down and shut up!" snarled Ratigan.

Just then Basil, Dawson, and Flaversham sped into
view.

"Faster!" shouted Ratigan to Fidget, who was madly pedaling the dirigible as Basil and his friends gained on them.

"Boss," Fidget wheezed, "we gotta lighten the load." He nodded at Olivia.

"Oh, you want to lighten the load?" said Ratigan. "What an excellent idea!" And with that, he knocked Fidget off the bike.

"*Aieeee!*" screamed Fidget as he went streaking through the air. Then there was a distant splash.

With Ratigan now pedaling, Basil's balloon drew even closer. Basil got ready to leap aboard the dirigible.

As he grabbed its underside, a desperate Ratigan tried to kick him off.

Suddenly Olivia screamed. Ratigan turned and gasped in horror. With a terrified Dawson and Flaversham looking on, the dirigible crashed smack into the face of the towering clock known as Big Ben!

When Basil recovered from the shock of the crash, he
realized that he was in the gears of the clock.

"Mr. Basil!" called a girl's voice. And out of the shadows
stepped Ratigan, clutching Olivia.

As Olivia struggled to free herself, a fight began between
Basil and Ratigan. Finally Ratigan dropped Olivia—right
onto a gear!

Basil rescued Olivia in the nick of time, and they scampered away. With lightning flashing behind him, Ratigan raced after them—through the gears, past some bells, and onto a beam.

As Ratigan closed in, Basil and Olivia escaped him by squeezing under some mesh.

But they had nowhere to go. In front of them was nothing but fog and rain. Behind them was Ratigan gnawing at the mesh.

Just then, the balloon pulled alongside. Basil hoisted Olivia while Dawson held onto Flaversham, who reached out and pulled his daughter to safety.

But at that very moment, Ratigan burst through the mesh. Basil was left to face his foe.

Tumbling off the steeple of Big Ben, Basil and Ratigan landed on one of the clock's hands.

"There's no escape this time," sneered Ratigan. "You've been beaten by my superior intelligence."

"You more intelligent than I?" said Basil. "What's 47,688 divided by 3,974?"

As Ratigan was finally giving his answer, the clock struck the hour. *Bong!* it went, and Ratigan lost his balance. He grabbed hold of Basil's cloak, but it ripped. The villainous Ratigan fell screaming into the fog.

At Basil's Baker Street flat, a grateful Flaversham and Olivia said their goodbyes to Basil and Dr. Dawson.

"Well," said Dawson. "Since this case is over, perhaps it's time I found a place to live...." But before he could finish his sentence, there was a knock at the door.

"Of course I'll take your case," Basil was saying. "Please meet Dr. Dawson who helps me with *all* my cases."

And that's how Dr. Dawson came to be Basil of Baker Street's trusted associate for many years to come.